The Fierce Little Woman and the Wicked Pirate

For my great-grandson Ethan with much love. J.C.

To Dave, for trying all the doors and windows. S.D.

Joy Cowley is one of New Zealand's best-loved
writers. She has won many awards for her work,
including the Distinguished Companion of the
NZ Order of Merit. Joy lives in Wellington,
New Zealand.

Sarah Davis grew up in New Zealand. She won
the 2009 Children's Book Council of Australia's
Crichton Award for Best New Illustrator. She lives
in Sydney, Australia.

This edition first published in 2010 by Gecko Press
PO Box 9335, Marion Square, Wellington 6141, New Zealand
info@geckopress.com

© Gecko Press 2010

Text © Joy Cowley 1984
Illustrations © Sarah Davis 2010

 Gecko Press acknowledges the generous
support of Creative New Zealand.

National Library of New Zealand Cataloguing-in-Publication Data

Cowley, Joy.
The fierce little woman and the wicked pirate / written by Joy Cowley;
illustrated by Sarah Davis.
Previously published: Auckland, N.Z. : Shortland Educational, 1984.
ISBN 978-1-87746-741-7 (hbk.)—ISBN 978-1-87746-740-0 (pbk.)
[1. Pirates—Fiction.] I. Davis, Sarah, 1971- II. Title.
NZ823.2—dc 22

Designed by Spencer Levine, Wellington, New Zealand
Printed by Everbest, China

For more curiously good books, visit www.geckopress.com

The Fierce Little Woman and the Wicked Pirate

By Joy Cowley

Illustrated by Sarah Davis

The fierce little woman lived in a house at the end of a jetty.
She knitted socks in blue and green wool, to sell
to sailors who had got their feet wet.

But when there were no ships at her jetty, she was quite alone.

Sometimes, the little woman walked up and down the jetty,
playing her bagpipes to the seagulls.

Inside her house, there was a trapdoor
which opened to the sea below.
In summer, the fierce little woman
climbed down through the trapdoor
to swim under the jetty.

In winter, she sat in her armchair beside the fire,
with a fishing line down the hole.
At night, she lay in bed, and listened to the sea
breathing in and out under her door.

One stormy day, a pirate came to the house on the jetty.

He stood on his toes, and started
tap-tap-tapping on the window.

The little woman was sitting in
her armchair, knitting fiercely.
'It's only the wind,' she said.

The pirate went on tap-tap-tapping at the glass.

The woman put her head on one side,
and listened. 'That's not the wind,' she said.
She looked at the window, and called,

'Who's there?'

A voice answered,

'I'm a wicked pirate.
Let me in.'

'No!' she said.

'I'm a fierce little woman, and you can't come in.
Go away, if you know what's good for you.'

'I'll break the window,'
said the pirate.

'You do, and I'll whack you
with my knitting needles,'
said the fierce little woman.

The pirate didn't answer.

A whole hour went by. Then there came
a knock-knock-knocking at the door.
A voice cried, 'Let me in!'

'I told you to go away!'
called the fierce little woman.

'Open your door, or I'll push it down,'
said the wicked pirate.

'Just you try it,' said the woman,
'and I'll hit you on the head
with my bagpipes.'

The pirate stopped knocking, and two hours passed.

The little woman listened. She could hear a faint
scratch-scratch-scratching under the floor.
'Let me in,' said the voice.
'Never!' she said.

'Raise the trapdoor!' said the pirate.
'If you don't, I'll force it open.'
'And you know what I'll do!' said the fierce little woman.
'I'll tie you up with my fishing line, and throw you into the sea.'

'You wouldn't!'
said the wicked pirate.
'Oh, yes I would!'
said the fierce little woman.

The pirate was quiet for a moment.

'Please let me in,' he said.
'My ship has gone without me,
and I've got no home. I'm hungry.
I've got wet feet. Worst of all,
it's getting dark.'

'No!'
she shouted.

'Oh, please, I beg you!' he said.

'I'm very scared of the dark.'

The little woman put down her knitting.

Very slowly, she opened the trapdoor, and the pirate came through, dripping seawater on the carpet.

She made him put his wet boots in front of the fire.
Then she gave him a new pair of blue and green socks.
'I didn't know a wicked pirate could be scared of the dark,'
she said.

The pirate wriggled his toes in the warm socks.
'I didn't know a fierce little woman could knit so fine,' he said.
'Or live in such a cosy house. Tell me, my fierce little woman...

'... would you consider being my wife?'

'Don't talk such nonsense,'
said the fierce little woman.
But for the first time in her life,

she smiled.

So the pirate and the little woman were married. They live in the house on the jetty, and now they have three children who are never fierce, and only sometimes wicked.

In summer, they all climb through the trapdoor to swim in the sea.

In winter, they sit by the fire
with fishing lines down the hole.

At night, they listen
to the sea breathing in and out
under the floor.

And once in a while …

... the little woman plays them
a lullaby on her bagpipes,
so they won't be scared of the dark.